GIANT OF THE SEA

A Story of a Sperm Whale

SMITHSONIAN OCEANIC COLLECTION

To Dad, Mom, Jamie and Mike with forever love — C.R.

To my wife, Kristen, for her love and support — S.G.

© 2002 Trudy Corporation and the Smithsonian Institution, Washington DC 20560.

Published by Soundprints Division of Trudy Corporation, Norwalk, Connecticut.

Book layout: Marcin D. Pilchowski
Editor: Laura Gates Galvin
Editorial assistance: Chelsea Shriver

First Edition 2002
10 9 8 7 6 5 4 3 2 1
Printed in Singapore

Acknowledgments:
    Our very special thanks to Dr. Richard W. Thorington Jr. of the Department of Systematic Biology at the Smithsonian Institution's National Museum of Natural History for his curatorial review.
    Soundprints would also like to thank Ellen Nanney and Robyn Bissette at the Smithsonian Institution's Office of Product Development and Licensing for their help in the creation of this book.

**Library of Congress Cataloging-in-Publication Data
is on file with the publisher and the Library of Congress.**

GIANT OF THE SEA

A Story of a Sperm Whale

by Courtney Granet Raff   Illustrated by Shawn Gould

4

On a bright and balmy day in Hawaii, a gentle wind blows across the soft, pink sand. Miles from the beach, below the surface of the sea, an enormous sperm whale and five others swim together.

Mama Whale gently rubs her body against her calf. Using her flipper, she touches the belly of another whale. Mama Whale is very close and connected to the members of her pod. The pod swims together. Soon, Mama Whale becomes hungry.

Mama Whale knows that she has to search for food deep below the sunny surface. She will need to make a very deep dive to get to her food. She prepares for the deep dive by first making a shallow dive. When she comes to the surface, she breathes through the blowhole at the top of her head. She dives and surfaces, again and again.

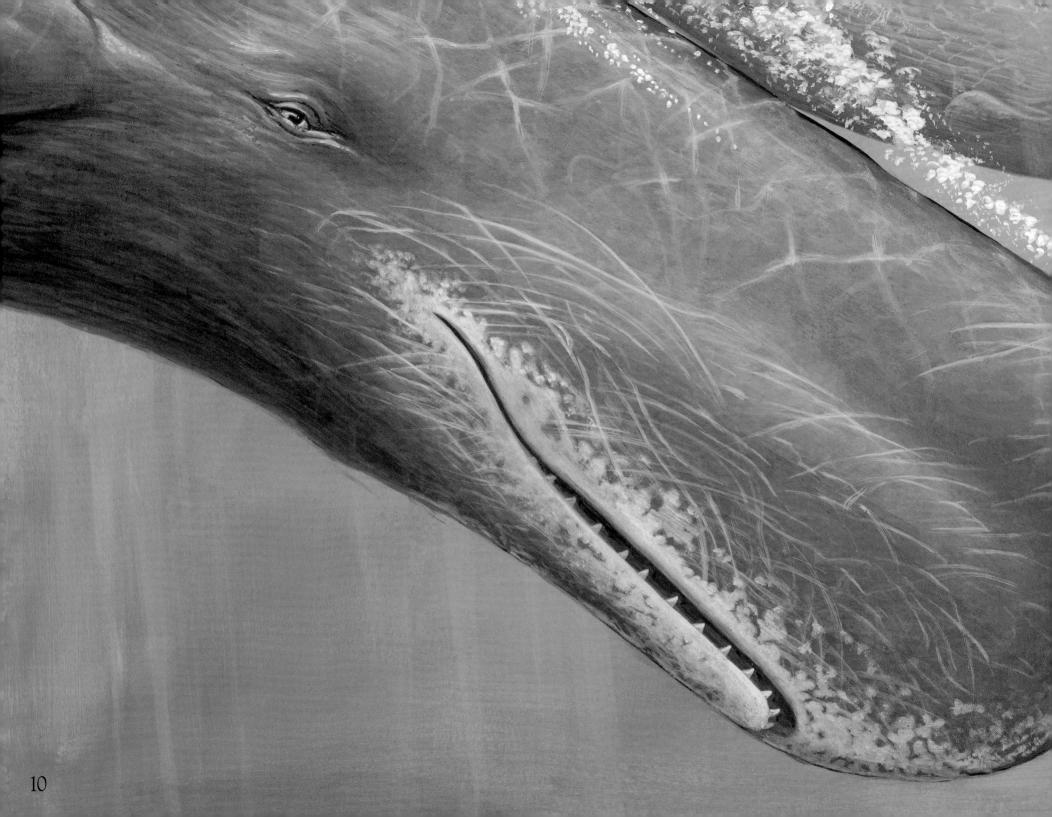

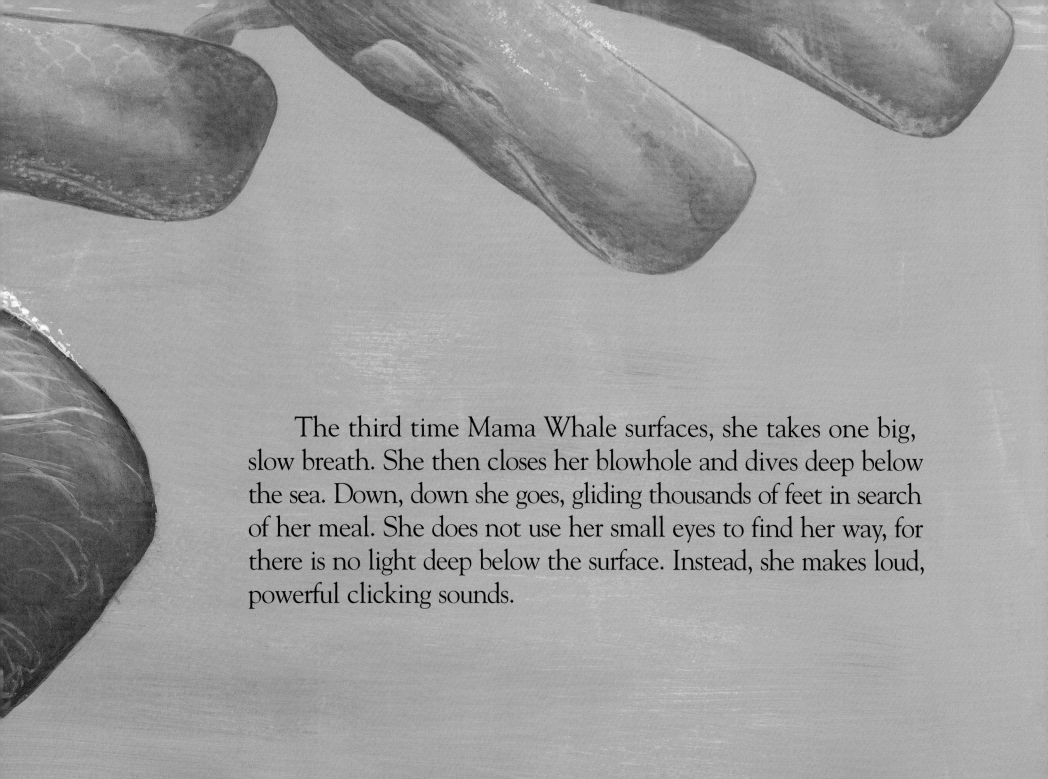

The third time Mama Whale surfaces, she takes one big, slow breath. She then closes her blowhole and dives deep below the sea. Down, down she goes, gliding thousands of feet in search of her meal. She does not use her small eyes to find her way, for there is no light deep below the surface. Instead, she makes loud, powerful clicking sounds.

The sounds Mama Whale makes bounce off anything near her, causing echoes all around. This is how she will find her food.

A school of fish swims in front of her. She senses the fish, but they are too small for her to eat. She continues her descent. Soon she senses another whale that she knows. They glide past each other.

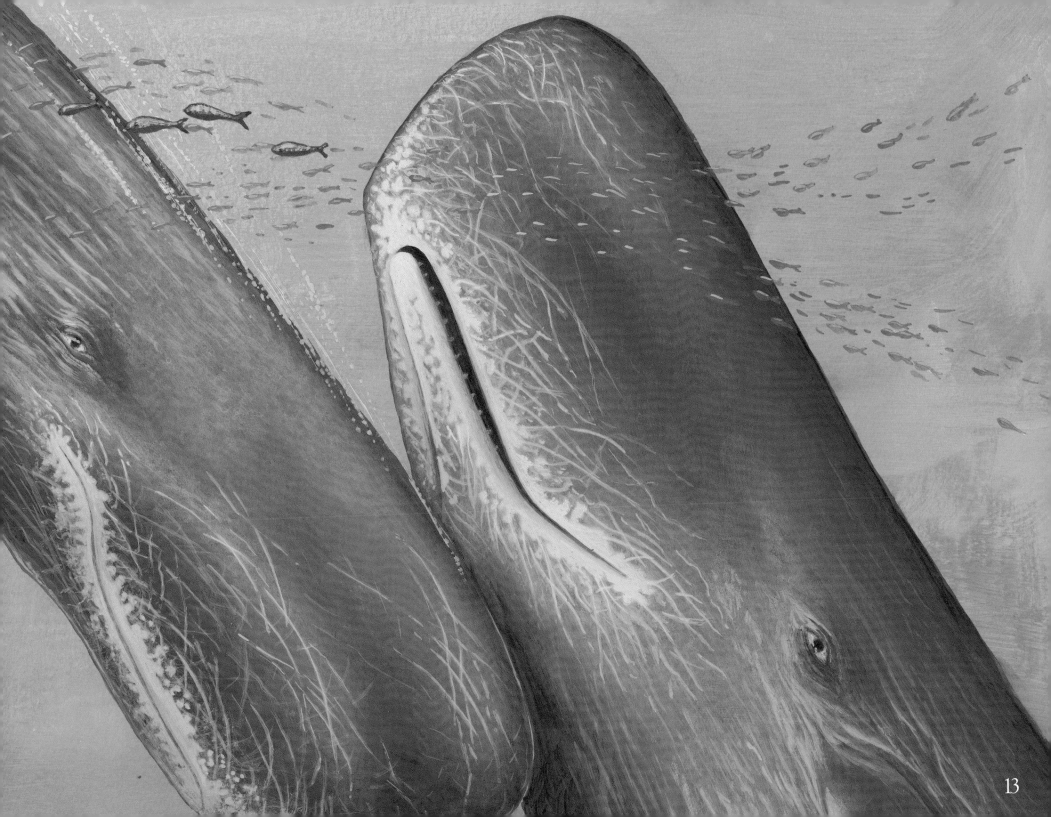

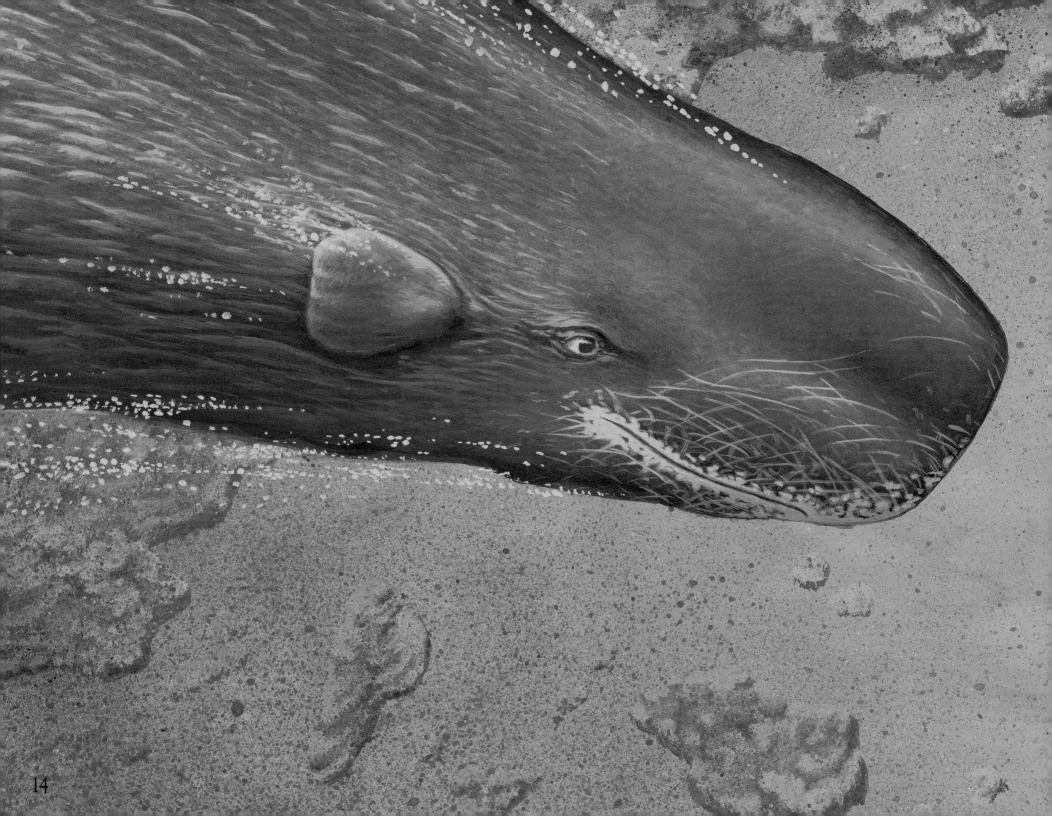

Mama Whale is now nearly half a mile below the surface. As she nears the ocean floor, she avoids sharp rocks and caves by carefully paying attention to the echoes around her. Mama Whale slows down. Echoes bounce back from her prey, a giant squid.

Mama Whale propels her body with her powerful fins and attacks the squid!

The surprised squid fights back, waving its arms and tentacles frantically, shooting a cloud of ink to scare Mama Whale. With one of its long tentacles, the squid strikes Mama Whale on her large head. But the strike does not stop Mama Whale.

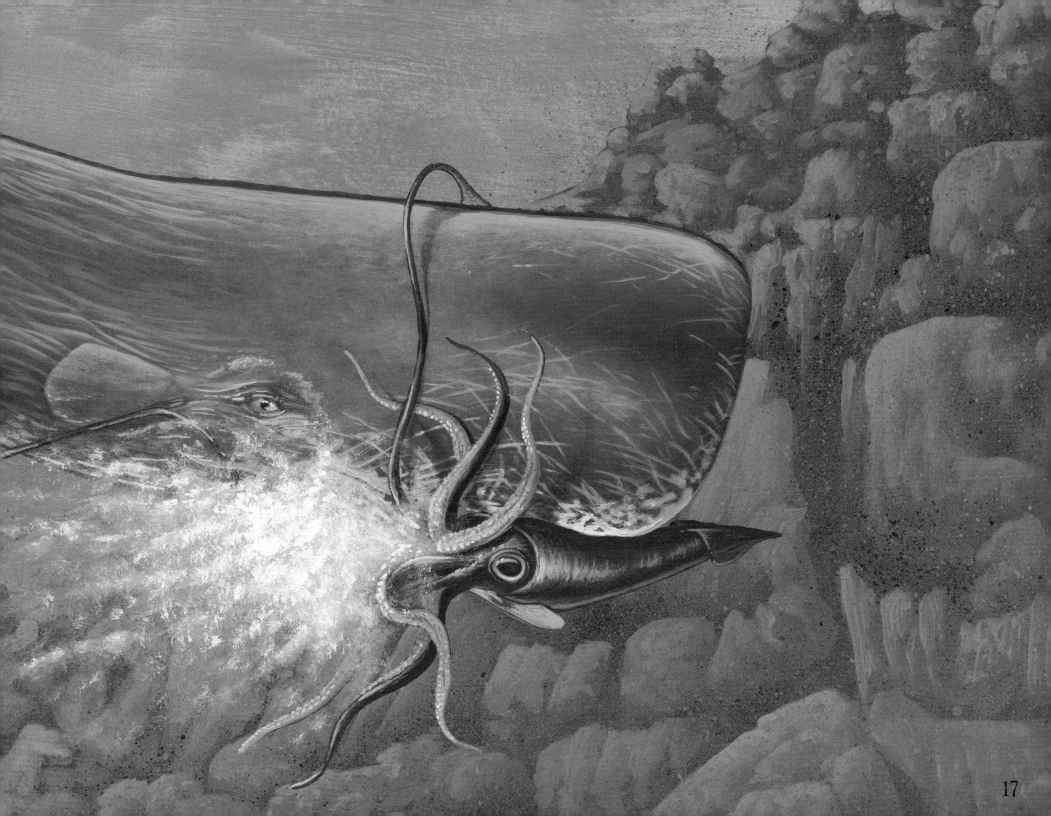

The squid tries to swim away but Mama Whale seizes it more firmly. Mama Whale opens her enormous mouth and grasps the squid with the fist-sized teeth that line her lower jaw. She then swallows the squid whole!

Mama Whale has been under water for almost an hour. She knows that she will have to breathe soon, so she turns around and glides back to the surface, relying on her powerful back fin to move her.

When she returns to the surface, she rejoins her calf and her pod. The female whales in her pod have been watching over her calf while she has been feeding.

Mama Whale is happy to see her calf. She rubs her gray fin along his underbelly. Mama Whale then rolls around. She is feeling frisky and playful, now that she has energy from her meal. Mama Whale thrusts her enormous body out of the water. She lands with a thunderous *splash* that can be heard for miles and miles!

23

Soon, Baby Whale tries it, too. *Splash! Crash! Bam!* This is fun for Mama Whale and Baby Whale. Four others join in the loud crashing of splashes. The entire pod plays together in the warm water. But before long Mama Whale's play is interrupted. She senses danger. There is a killer whale peeking his head up from a distance!

The killer whale has his eye on Baby Whale, who has strayed from
the pod. Mama Whale stops her play and swims over to Baby Whale.
The other whales quickly join her to help protect Baby Whale. The pod
makes a circle around Baby Whale. Their bodies are submerged and their
huge tails are facing out. Whales use their tails as weapons.

The slick killer whale swims much faster than Mama Whale. He slyly moves his black and white body around the circle of whale giants. He persists for a while because he knows that the calf would make a perfect afternoon meal. He swims around and around the circle of whales, but he knows that he cannot penetrate the pods' defense. Eventually, he gives up.

29

When the killer whale swims away, Mama Whale knows that Baby Whale is no longer in danger, for now. She nudges the frightened calf to reassure him that he is safe.

It has been a long day for Mama Whale. She is ready to rest. The sky darkens as the sun goes down. Mama Whale floats beneath the purple sunset. She will take short naps throughout the night, for she must remember to breathe and keep her calf safe.

About the Sperm Whale

Sperm whales are the largest of the toothed whales. They are easily recognizable, yet rarely visible. They have square-shaped heads that are one-third the size of their bodies.

Sperm whales get their name from *spermaceti*, the oil that is found in their enormous heads. This oil becomes waxy when it is cold and has historically been coveted by whalers. The famous story *Moby Dick* is about a whaler and a sperm whale.

Sperm whales can be found in all oceans of the world, except in polar areas. They are also the deepest divers of all whales and can remain underwater for as long as 90 minutes. They are hunters and use a highly developed sense of clicks called echolocation to find their prey, which consists of squid, octopus, fish and eel.

Sperm whales are social animals that travel in pods of females and calves. The males come to the tropical waters to mate with the females in the winter for a short period of time. Sperm whales communicate with one another by using a complex system of clicks called codas.

Sperm whales breathe through their blowholes. When they exhale, their blow is projected forward and to the left, which is unique among whales.

Glossary

blowhole: The opening of the nostril through which air is inhaled and exhaled. It is found on the top of the head.

calf: A baby sperm whale.

fins: Broad, steering or propelling appendages. Fins are used for movement and protection. The sperm whale's two tail fins are called flukes.

flippers: The small, flat "arms or legs" of the sperm whale that are used for steering and balance.

pod: A group of whales that swim, feed, play and rest together.

tentacle: One of eight "arms" of a squid or octopus.

Points of Interest in This Book

pp. 4-5: Hawaiian island.
pp. 12-13: a school of fish.
pp. 14-15: giant squid.

pp. 16-17: giant squid ink.
pp. 28-29: Orca (killer whale).